Meet . . .

Rob, our h... His f...

...arsha

. . . and Rob's neighbours,

Mr Vork

Mrs Vork

Their son, Norman

And the baby, Petal

Not to mention a passing spaceship . . .

Jeremy Strong once worked in a bakery, putting the jam into three thousand doughnuts every night. Now he puts the jam in stories instead, which he finds much more exciting. At the age of three, he fell out of a first-floor bedroom window and landed on his head. His mother says that this damaged him for the rest of his life and refuses to take any responsibility. He loves writing stories because he says it is 'the only time you alone have complete control and can make anything happen'. His ambition is to make you laugh (or at least snuffle). Jeremy Strong lives near Bath with his wife, Gillie, four cats and a flying cow.

Are you feeling silly enough to read more?

**THE BATTLE FOR CHRISTMAS
THE BEAK SPEAKS
BEWARE! KILLER TOMATOES
CHICKEN SCHOOL
DINOSAUR POX
GIANT JIM AND THE HURRICANE
THE HUNDRED-MILE-AN-HOUR DOG
KRAZY COW SAVES THE WORLD – WELL, ALMOST
LOST! THE HUNDRED-MILE-AN-HOUR DOG
MY BROTHER'S FAMOUS BOTTOM
MY BROTHER'S HOT CROSS BOTTOM
THERE'S A PHARAOH IN OUR BATH!**

**JEREMY STRONG'S
LAUGH-YOUR-SOCKS-OFF JOKE BOOK**

LAUGH YOUR SOCKS OFF WITH
Jeremy STRONG

I'm Telling You They're ALIENS

Illustrated by
Nick Sharratt

PUFFIN

PUFFIN BOOKS

Published by the Penguin Group
Penguin Books Ltd, 80 Strand, London WC2R 0RL, England
Penguin Group (USA) Inc., 375 Hudson Street, New York, New York 10014, USA
Penguin Group (Canada), 90 Eglinton Avenue East, Suite 700, Toronto, Ontario, Canada M4P 2Y3
(a division of Pearson Penguin Canada Inc.)
Penguin Ireland, 25 St Stephen's Green, Dublin 2, Ireland (a division of Penguin Books Ltd)
Penguin Group (Australia), 250 Camberwell Road, Camberwell, Victoria 3124, Australia
(a division of Pearson Australia Group Pty Ltd)
Penguin Books India Pvt Ltd, 11 Community Centre, Panchsheel Park, New Delhi – 110 017, India
Penguin Group (NZ), 67 Apollo Drive, Rosedale, North Shore 0632, New Zealand
(a division of Pearson New Zealand Ltd)
Penguin Books (South Africa) (Pty) Ltd, 24 Sturdee Avenue, Rosebank, Johannesburg 2196, South Africa

Penguin Books Ltd, Registered Offices: 80 Strand, London WC2R 0RL, England

puffinbooks.com

First published in Puffin Books 2000
This edition published 2009
1

Text copyright © Jeremy Strong, 2000
Illustrations copyright © Nick Sharratt, 2000
All rights reserved

The moral right of the author and illustrator has been asserted

Set in Baskerville MT
Made and printed in England by Clays Ltd, St Ives plc

British Library Cataloguing in Publication Data
A CIP catalogue record for this book is available from the British Library

ISBN: 978-0-141-32442-5

www.greenpenguin.co.uk

Mixed Sources
Product group from well-managed
forests and other controlled sources
www.fsc.org Cert no. SA-COC-1592
© 1996 Forest Stewardship Council

Penguin Books is committed to a sustainable future
for our business, our readers and our planet.
The book in your hands is made from paper
certified by the Forest Stewardship Council.

Contents

1 What's in a Name?

OK, I admit it – I worry. I worry a lot. I *like* worrying. If I'm not worried about anything then that worries me.

Take corners. I mean, they're nasty things. You never know what's lurking round a corner. There could be an escaped rhinoceros, a mad-axe murderer – maybe even a gateway into a parallel universe, one-way only.

When I was six I made myself a really neat gadget. I got a bamboo stick and taped a mirror to the end of it, at an angle. When I walked to school, I would hold it out in front of me and take a good peek round any corners, making sure it was safe round there.

Stopping at every corner did slow things down a bit though. It took hours to reach school and it drove my mum mad.

It didn't take long for everyone at school to discover how worried I was either. On my very first day, when the bell started clanging for morning play, I was out of my seat in a flash and racing for the door. 'Fire! Fire! We're all going to die!'

Before Miss Drew could stop us, the whole class was panicking: leaping out of seats, sending chairs flying, scrambling over tables to escape, and shouting and screaming and yelling for mummy. I mean, just imagine it for yourself – a class full of four and five year olds all trying to save themselves from a non-existent inferno.

Miss Drew was mown down by a pack of terrified infants, and it was only the appearance of the headteacher, backed up by the caretaker, the secretary, and three dinner ladies that stopped a tidal wave of teeny toddlers engulfing the school. Somehow they managed to round us up and calm us down, although the headteacher did have to climb up a ladder to pluck me from the tree I had zoomed up for safety. The extraordinary thing was that nobody was cross with me. They seemed to think it was an easy mistake to make.

The trouble was, and still is, that I do worry. I just have this feeling that won't go away, a feeling that some kind of disaster is out there waiting to happen to me. I'm eleven now, and I still worry, and I still use my mirror-stick when I think nobody is looking.

At school they think I'm weird. They aren't nasty or anything, although they do laugh at me and they don't usually want to play with me. I could count the number of friends I have on one hand with no fingers held up. In other words, zero.

You see, it's not just the worrying, it's the other things. Like my name.

Robert Smith, that's me. I know what you're thinking. What's wrong with Robert Smith? OK then, try this out for size – Robert *Wolfgang Amadeus* Smith. That's right, Wolfgang Amadeus. My parents like classical music. Their favourite composer is Mozart, so they gave me his names. Nice

one, Mum, nice one, Dad. I really love you
too. I'll tell you one thing: when I grow up
(if I survive that long), I will NOT give my
children daft names like Wolfgang Amadeus.

And there's something else too: I'm the
only boy in my class learning the violin.
Well, it was Mum and Dad's idea. I think
they are secretly hoping that I will turn into
a real Wolfgang Amadeus, although I don't
really fancy turning into somebody who's
been dead for more than two hundred years.
For a start, Mozart wore a wig, and
knickerbockers and stockings. Can you
imagine me turning up at school dressed like
that? I don't think so!

To tell you the truth, I do like playing the
violin. It's just that most of the boys in my
class seem to find it amusing. They think
I'm different, but we're all different really,
aren't we? I mean we all have funny little
things that we do or think or like, things we
never dare tell anyone in case they laugh at
us or think we're stupid. So we keep very
quiet and hope they never find out. (I used
to know a boy who never put just one piece
of rubbish into a rubbish bin. He always put

in two pieces so that the two pieces could talk to each other, and wouldn't get lonely.)

My problem is that a violin case is a bit obvious. It attracts attention, and you can't pretend it's anything else. If people come up to you and say, 'Hey, is that a violin you're carrying?' you can hardly say, 'No, it's a collapsible mountain bike.'

As you can tell, I do have a few problems, and the problems are mostly with me, myself. There's not much I can do about that. I can't suddenly *stop* liking music, or stop worrying for that matter. I can't just change myself. This is how I am. But I do have things that help me get by.

One of the best is a brilliant CD Rom that I use all the time on my computer. It's called 'Your Horoscope For the Next Fifty Years'. It tells me what to expect every day, which can be very worrying. You spend the rest of the day waiting for dreadful things to happen.

Last Tuesday was pretty embarrassing. I went through the astrological predictions for the day on the computer and it said the world would end at twenty-three minutes past eleven because an asteroid was going to smash into Planet Earth. (Mind you, it did give a horoscope for the next day, and the day after that, and the day after that . . . which is a bit weird when you think about it. I mean, if the world's just been destroyed by an asteroid, you can hardly have a future, can you?)

I warned everyone at school, and would they listen? Of course not. At twenty-*two* minutes past eleven we were in the middle of maths and I climbed underneath my desk. Everyone ignored me, they always do, even Mrs Ashworth, who teaches me now. She just rolled her eyes and let me get on with it. They're used to it, you see. Twenty-three minutes past eleven arrived, but the asteroid didn't. I gave it another five minutes in case the classroom clock was fast and then crawled out, sat on my seat and got on with my maths. Nobody said a word.

Want to know what they call me at school? *Chicken Licken.* I'm sure you're familiar with the story of Chicken Licken. Chicken Licken is (guess what!) a chicken. One day he is asleep beneath an oak tree and an acorn falls on his head. He jumps up, terribly worried, because he thinks the sky is falling down. He goes racing round the countryside telling all the other animals, 'The sky's falling down! The sky's falling down! We're all going to die!' Soon everyone is rushing about, convinced that they're going to perish because the sky's collapsing.

Does it remind you of anything – like my first day at school and the bell going off? I remember the afternoon Miss Drew read the story of Chicken Licken to the class, and everyone, and I mean *everyone*, turned and stared at me. It was instant recognition. They've called me Chicken Licken ever since. They all think I'm a complete waste of space.

And then the aliens came.

2 Strange Beings

Today's horoscope: An excellent day! You can let yourself relax. The heat is taken off you at work, and you will be surprised at how easily the day passes.

Hmmm. That is truly what it said. I remember it clearly. Well, I suppose nobody can be right all the time, not even Mystic Myrtle, the Cosmic Turtle. (Just in case you were wondering, that's my CD Rom program. The astrological charts are presented by this giant, galaxy-cruising turtle. It's got really good graphics.) Anyhow, my horoscope was not exactly accurate because this was the day the new neighbours arrived.

The house across the road had been empty for weeks. We were beginning to wonder if anyone would move in.

'You're keeping them away with your violin practice,' said Dad, and he made squeaky-squeak noises and grinned at me. It was meant to be a joke, his *one* joke, and he repeated it just about every day. Even Mum was getting fed up with it.

Then suddenly *BAMM!* We'd got new neighbours. It was like they'd fallen out of space and landed in the house next door.

Which is almost exactly what had happened.

I knew they were aliens the first moment I saw them. I could feel it in my body. I got this kind of creeping sensation, as if ants were slowly crawling up and down the inside of my bones. You know how when you see an old bone, it's all sort of hollow down the middle, like a tunnel? Well, that's where these ants were crawling, up and down, and it worried me.

Nobody had seen a removal van. Nobody had seen the new neighbours move in. One moment they weren't there, and the next moment they were. It was just like *Star Trek*, you know, when they get beamed from one place to another. Only nobody saw it happen.

I was in my bedroom doing my violin practice when I noticed him. He looked like a typical human, but, I mean, what a give-away! Aliens coming to our planet *always* look like ordinary humans, otherwise you'd spot them a mile off and go around screaming 'Help! Aliens! Aliens invading Planet Earth!' (Well, I would anyhow.)

He looked about fourteen. He was lanky and there was something threatening about the way he just stood there. He was wearing shorts, the really baggy kind that come down past your knees. He had funny hair too. Well, it wasn't exactly funny. *Weird* would be a better word. It was very short, and it had a zigzag pattern shaved into it, as if the hairdresser had had some terrifying scare and his electric razor had slipped.

I guess it was because his hair was so short that his ears stuck out. They were extraordinary. They sat on the sides of his head like twin satellite dishes. I mean, with ears like those he could pick up messages from deep space, let alone satellite TV.

Anyhow, by this time, I had goose pimples all over, which is a sure sign that I was seriously scared. I was staring down at this boy and then his mother came out and called to him. She was pretty and well-dressed, but she looked even more worried than me, as if she had some dreadful secret – which she did, of course. There was something else too.

She had The Mark *upon her.*

There was a dark blotch just below her throat. I could tell it wasn't a bruise or anything like that. I zipped downstairs, borrowed Dad's bird-watching binoculars and zoomed in. You know what that mark was? It was a star cluster, a constellation! She might just as well have carried a sticker on her head, with the name of her planet written on it.

She called to the boy and he went across to her. She whispered something to him and they both gazed about as if they were keeping an eye out for something, and their heads made this curious sharp movement –

they looked more like birds or lizards than human beings. I mean, you know, it was *strange*. I kept out of sight behind my curtains. The mother pointed to the watch on the boy's wrist and he nodded several times. Then they went indoors.

By this time those ants had invaded every bone in my body. I knew for certain that I had just had a Close Encounter of the Third Kind – the kind where you come face to face with a real alien. I had to sit down. I can't take aliens standing up, not straight away at any rate. I sat down on my bed and I was sweating and breathing hard. The goose pimples had gone, but now my skin was going hot and cold. This was a sure sign of a fever. I was burning up!

I've got this really useful book which I use in just such emergencies. I seized *The Complete Medical Encyclopedia* and skimmed through the pages. It didn't take me long to work out that I was well into the second stage of malaria. Malaria – The Curse of the Jungle! But I hadn't been anywhere near a jungle. The closest thing to a jungle in my area were the bushes in our front garden, and they were not exactly infested with malaria-carrying mosquitoes.

There was only one possible answer. The aliens had brought it with them! This was no ordinary kind of malaria. This was more like Inter-Galactic Malaria, the most deadly kind there could possibly be, with NO KNOWN CURE AND I WAS THE VERY FIRST VICTIM!

I began to wonder how long I had to live. Would my next breath be my last? My throat felt all raspy. My legs had gone weak at the knees. I grabbed a pen and some paper and hastily began scribbling a note.

Dear World,

I have been killed by a deadly virus brought by aliens living in the house opposite. Be very careful! Do not enter their house without protective clothing. You have been warned!
Love, Robert.
P.S. I told you this would happen!

The 'Love, Robert' at the end seemed a

bit wimpy, but what else could I put? Anyway, what would you have done? Just think for a moment. Do you go and tell your parents?

It would be like, 'Mum, aliens have moved in over the road.'

'Oh dear, that is a shame. Make sure you keep your curtains pulled, and wear clean underpants.' (Mum is always telling me to wear clean underpants, in case I have an accident. 'I don't want you ending up in hospital with dirty underwear,' she says. Well, *I* don't want to end up in hospital, full stop!)

The trouble is people think you're very strange if you go round saying things about alien invasions, and if you're not very careful they come and take you away and lock you up and feed you on things like rice pudding (which I hate).

So who do you tell? Do you go to the police? Do you tell the kids in your class? They already think I'm half-mad anyway, and they wouldn't listen to me anyhow, not after that episode with the non-existent asteroid.

I decided to keep quiet. I thought I'd keep a low profile, pretend there was nothing wrong, but all the time be on the lookout, watching for clues. I had already discovered that there were four of them altogether and now I had to find out what kind of aliens they were and why they had come to Planet Earth.

Actually the answer to that question was pretty obvious. Aliens only come to Earth for one reason, and that is to take it over, to invade every bit of it. Everyone knows that. I mean, they're not likely to drive halfway across the universe just to ask if they can borrow some sugar.

By this time you will probably have worked out for yourself that I hadn't taken my last breath and died, otherwise I wouldn't be able to write this down for you. Evidently the aliens were not going to use a deadly virus. They had some other plan up their sleeve . . . assuming aliens have sleeves. If they don't, then what can they hide things up? Their nostrils? Armpits? Ears? I seem to be going off-track here a bit.

You can imagine my surprise, and my

rampaging feelings, when Mum made the following announcement, shortly after lunch. 'I've met the new neighbours,' she said. 'They seem nice. I've asked them over for a cup of coffee this afternoon, so we can meet the family.'

The aliens were coming to our house – for tea and biscuits!

'How many are there?' Dad asked warily. He doesn't like having to make conversation with strangers.

'There's Norman and Petal and the parents. I don't know their first names, but their surname is Vork.'

'Vork!' Dad gave a short laugh, but it wasn't funny to me. It was just so obvious. Aliens were bound to have strange names. I mean – Vork – it was probably an alien word. It probably meant *Death to all Earthlings*, or *Killer-king of Krargg* or something.

Mum raised her eyebrows. 'That's what they said. I don't suppose they think their surname is funny at all. I hope you won't laugh at them when they come over.'

'Mum, he wears shorts,' I said.

'Just right for this weather. You should do the same. Get some air up your legs.'

'Mum!'

'You are a bit weedy, Robert. You should get more exercise, eat more.'

I was silent. The conversation was rapidly moving into *What's Wrong with Robert: Stage One*. This is the bit where my parents say I need building up. *Stage Two* is when they suggest I take up weight training. *Stage Three* arrives when they start talking about high protein diets, fitness programmes and no more watching TV.

'What's Mr Vork like?' asked Dad, and I inwardly sighed with relief. I'd escaped being turned into Muscle-man for the time being.

'Oh, he seemed a bit quiet, but he's got sharp eyes.'

'Sharp?'

'Yes, they bore into you, you know? Penetrating eyes, and they dart all over the place.' (Have you ever noticed how people say really daft things? How can anyone's eyes *dart* about? They're not fish.)

Dad asked what Mr Vork did for a living.

'Something to do with computers, that's what his wife said. Rob, you know Norman's only fourteen? You could be friends.'

'With someone called Norman? Nobody's called Norman.'

'Norman is,' said Dad, laughing at his own joke. 'Anyhow, you can't write someone off just because of their name.'

Oh yeah! Tell me another! What about Wolfgang Amadeus then, eh? What about that? Besides, Norman was *fourteen*. It was like Mum was asking me to be friends with a werewolf. My parents know *nothing*.

'Are you listening, Robert?'

'What?'

Mum gave a big sigh. 'World of your own,' she murmured. 'I said, just be nice to him when he comes over this afternoon, and little Petal too. She's only a year and a half old. She looked rather sweet.'

How could my parents be taken in so easily?

3 Even Closer Encounters

'She can talk already!' cried Mum, and I thought, *Of course she can talk. She's an alien. She can probably speak a thousand languages, and come to think of it, she's probably got a thousand different tongues to speak them with.* But Mum was still going all gooey.

'Goodness, Robert didn't learn to talk until he was almost three.' Thank you, Mum.

'Is it unusual?' asked Mrs Vork anxiously, as if she didn't want anyone to think her daughter was any different to other children, and no wonder. I fixed Mrs Vork with my best *I-know-what-you're-up-to* kind of stare, and I got a really good peek at that star sign. It was made up of twelve stars, in some weird shape, with little lines joining them up round the edges, like a dot-to-dot picture.

'Robert, is there something wrong with your neck?'

I straightened up, and Mrs Vork threw me a panicky glance. Oh yes! I'd got her worried all right – but not half as worried as she'd got me. I mean, she was an alien. You know what they're like. They have laser eyes and stuff. I was pretty sure that the Vorks wouldn't attempt anything yet. They would be more concerned about their master-plan to take over the world.

'I was wondering if I might borrow some sugar,' said Mrs Vork and I couldn't help myself. I just had to laugh. I mean, this was so obvious! Everyone turned and looked at me and the whole room went deadly quiet.

'Sorry,' I muttered. I felt my skin go prickly and flush strawberry from head to toe.

'Of course you can have some sugar,' said Mum, and then she began gurgling at little Petal, 'She's so clever!' before going into ecstasies over the baby's amazing intelligence yet again.

'That's nothing,' muttered Norman. 'I could talk when I was eleven months.'

'No you couldn't,' said Mr Vork, fixing his eyes on his son.

'Oh yes I . . . couldn't.' Norman turned away sulkily from his father's threatening gaze. His dad had extraordinary eyebrows, like fat, black caterpillars.

'Gimme more,' cried Petal, making a grab for the chocolate cake that Mum had placed on the table.

'Just look at her!' smiled Dad. I thought, *Yeah, just look at her. What a greedy pig.*

'What a greedy pig,' said Norman.

'Norman!'

'That's what Robert thinks, and I agree with him.'

I was astonished. 'How did you know what I was thinking?' Norman just snorted back at me.

Mum glanced anxiously at everyone. She did want things to go well. 'Robert, why don't you take Norman upstairs and show him your computer or your violin while we talk to Mr and Mrs Vork.'

I was quite pleased about this. It would be

a chance to study this alien creature more closely. When we got to my bedroom he went straight across to my computer. It was time to ask a few probing questions.

'Did you really know what I was thinking?'

'Nope.'

'But I *was* thinking she was a pig.'

'Everyone thinks she's a pig,' said Norman. 'And anyhow, I *could* talk when I was eleven months, so there. It's no big deal. Does this computer have a copier?'

'A what?'

'A copier, you know, for copying things.'

'Oh! You mean like a photocopier?'

Norman gave me a weird look, as if I was truly stupid. 'Of course not, Jellyhead,' he sneered. 'I mean like copying living things. Dogs, cats, elephants . . .'

'You've got a computer that can do that?' Inside, you can bet my mind was going boggle-boggle, but I tried to stay calm. This was like an actual admission. I mean, short of him actually saying 'I am an alien,' this was it!

But Norman was getting bored. He

seemed to think that my computer was hopelessly out of date. 'My dad's in computers,' he said. 'He knows more about computers than anyone in the universe.'

'I bet he does.' I tried to sound cutting.

'Yours is rubbish.' Now that *was* cutting. I shrank back on to the bed.

Norman kept glancing round the room. Eventually he spotted my violin. 'Can you play that thing?'

'Sort of.'

'Go on then.'

I picked it up and began to play a little piece I'd been working on. The effect it had on Norman was incredible. He kind of doubled up, with his hands pressed to his head. He toppled over to one side and began writhing about on the floor.

'Oh come on!' I protested. 'My playing isn't *that* bad.' I put the violin down and Norman struggled to his feet. He stared at the little wooden instrument.

'That is an instrument of torture,' he croaked.

'You must have heard a violin before,' I said.

'Not played like that.' He sat on my bed. 'What do you do up here all day? I've never been in such a boring room.'

'What's special about your bedroom then?'

Norman grinned at me. 'For a start I've got an electric guitar and amplifiers,' he boasted. 'And I've got *two* computers, three games' decks, and my room is twice as big as yours. I've got a satellite tracker and everything.'

A satellite tracker? What a give-away! This was getting scary. I began wishing that Norman would go.

'I must get back,' muttered Norman. 'It's getting late.'

He'd done it again! Read my thoughts! By this time I didn't just have goose pimples; they were more like elephant pimples.

Norman hurried downstairs. His parents were fussing about too, all of them saying that they must get going, despite Mum's offer of another cup of coffee.

'Really must rush,' insisted Mr Vork. 'Things to do.'

'How did you two boys get on?' asked Mrs Vork.

'He tried to kill me with his violin,' Norman muttered, and my dad laughed.

'Robert does that to everyone,' he said. 'He's going to join the army when he gets older. You know, secret weapon!' My dad can be so witty.

Mr Vork gave a faint smile. I don't think he realized it was meant to be a joke. He seemed almost . . . edgy. He scratched at the open collar of his shirt. My eyes almost fell out of my head. There it was again – *The Mark*! He had exactly the same star cluster, in the same place.

'We must go,' said Mr Vork, tapping his watch.

'Of course. You must have a lot of unpacking to do,' agreed Dad.

'Unpacking?'

'From moving in.'

'Yes, of course. Come on, Mrs Vork, Norman, we must go unpacking.'

The new neighbours almost ran across the road to their own house and vanished inside.

'Strange people,' said Dad. 'He called his own wife Mrs Vork, as if she was a stranger.'

'She forgot the sugar,' said Mum. Trust

her to fret over the really important issues.

After the Vorks had gone, I started doing some fretting of my own. I was worried. Could Norman really tell what I was thinking? I know he'd said he couldn't, but then he would say that, wouldn't he? And if Norman had this power, did that mean *all the Vorks knew what we were all thinking*?

There was something else nagging me too. If they were aliens, then what were they really like? Obviously their human form was just a disguise. What did they look like when they were not playing at being human? And why were they in such a rush to get home? I gazed out of the window, across the road, towards their house. I could see the slowly setting sun reflected in their windows.

And then all at once it came to me. Dracula! They were like vampires. You know how vampires are only vampires at night? During the daytime they have to hide. Maybe these creatures from outer space were like that, only they had to hide by night, because at night-time . . . *they changed into their real alien forms!*

And there I was on one side of the street,

while on the other side there were four
aliens poised to take over the world.

This was Big-time Worrying.

4 Bogbrush

Today's horoscope: New friends bring excitement into your life. Beware of yellow.

How I managed to get any sleep I don't know, but when I got up the next day I began to realize that this was a problem I could not tackle on my own. I needed help, and the only place I could get help was from school. So before school started, I went round the playground talking to everyone from my class.

'Listen,' I said. 'We've got new neighbours, and they're creatures from the furthest reaches of space, and they are going to invade Earth. We've got to stop them.

Will you help me?'

'Not again!' said most of them. 'Rob, you thought aliens were coming six months ago. Let's face it, Rob, the only strange creature living in your street is you.'

Others just said, 'Hey! Great game! Can my friend play as well?' I told them it wasn't a game, and they looked at me sadly. 'You mean you *really* think there are aliens living next to you?' Then they would sigh and walk off with their hands in their pockets.

Some people just laughed straight off. Kevin Durbell threw his arms into the air and screamed, 'Argh! Chicken Licken's being attacked by aliens! Run for your lives!' And he ran round the playground yelling and pulling stupid faces. I reckon Kevin Durbell is about as funny as poo on your shoe.

As for everyone else, they seemed more interested in the fact that the school had been broken into overnight and all the computers and TVs had been nicked. 'No TV to watch!' they moaned, as if it was the end of the world. And all the time I knew

how the world really would end if they
didn't help me.

How many helpers do you think I got?
How many brave warriors signed up to fight
the aliens and save the world?

None.

I was going to have to fight them alone.

That is how things stood until lunchtime.
Then Bogbrush turned up. Bogbrush is not
her real name of course. Bogbrush's real
name is Marsha and that's partly how she
got her name. You know – marsh, bog?
They mean the same thing, don't they? So
when the other kids (Kevin Durbell mostly)
heard that her name was Marsha they used
every bit of imagination in their tiny brains
and came up with Bogbrush. I mean, kids
can be so inventive sometimes.

You can probably tell that I get a bit fed
up with nicknames. Chicken Licken doesn't
exactly send me into ecstasies of delight.

Anyhow, at lunchtime I was standing in
the playground by myself, as usual – if I go
and stand next to anybody they usually
move away pretty quickly, and I knew that
today they all thought I had gone off my

trolley completely – when Bogbrush came wandering over and stood silently next to me. She's bigger than me, a whole head taller, and she's gangly and awkward and has long, thin arms, and legs like sticks that she keeps tripping over.

I don't suppose I'm giving you a very good impression of her, am I? I'm making her sound weird. But she is a bit like that: tall and thin, with vague eyes and she's got this big mop of unruly hair, all curls. That's the brush bit of course. Bogbrush.

And there she was, offering her help. It was going to be me and Bogbrush against the mighty force of the aliens. My heart sank into my boots. My right-hand man was a woman! (Well, a girl at any rate.)

'What are they like?' she asked, and my spirits gave a small leap. I have to say a *small* leap because after all she was a girl, and a rather weird one at that. Like me, Bogbrush is a bit of a loner. I remembered my horoscope. *A new friend . . . beware of yellow.* The new friend had to be Marsha and as for the warning, that was so obvious.

'I think they've got yellow skin, but I haven't seen them properly yet.'

'How do you know they're extraterrestrials?'

'Come back to my house this afternoon and you'll see why.'

'Anyhow,' she continued, 'they won't be aliens. Those things always turn out to be hoaxes. People said they'd found an alien on a beach a few years ago. You know what it was? The dead, decaying body of a giant squid, washed up from the bottom of the ocean.'

'My new neighbours are not giant squid,' I muttered angrily. 'And besides, they've got stellar markings on their throats.'

'Really?' Marsha seemed a fraction more interested.

'The man and the woman have the same sign. It's a group of stars.'

Marsha sat down next to me and studied my face carefully. 'Which group?'

'How am I supposed to know that?'

She paused, deep in thought. 'It could be Upsilon Andromedae. That's got a solar system.'

'You mean other planets?'

'Yes. Three planets have been discovered already, maybe more. Trouble is, Upsilon is forty-four light years away from Earth.' This was astonishing. I mean, Bogbrush was weird, but I had no idea she was into astronomy. 'They'd have to have overcome light-speed to get here, and that's supposed to be impossible. *Supposed to be*,' she repeated, 'although I have my own pet theory on that one.' She frowned at her feet. 'Why do you think there are only four of them?'

'I don't know. I suppose there could be more, spread across other cities, right across the world, a network of aliens, preparing . . .' The skin on the back of my neck prickled. I was beginning to scare myself. Bogbrush glanced down at me and gave a little sigh.

'You worry too much,' she said. 'Suppose they've come in peace?' I shuffled my feet. Bogbrush had a point. It just didn't feel right though. I was certain those aliens were a threat, perhaps the most evil threat the Earth had ever faced.

'So why have you decided to help?' I asked.

'I'm bored.'

Oh great! That was *so* encouraging! My only ally had joined up through boredom.

I took Bogbrush back to my house after school. Mum raised her eyebrows. It was lucky Dad wasn't there. He would certainly have said something really witty, like 'Got a girlfriend?'

We went up to my bedroom, pulled a couple of chairs over to the window and stared at the house over the road. Nothing happened for a while. Mum brought us up some drinks and biscuits. Bogbrush began to wander round my room, poking her nose into everything.

'You've got a computer,' she said.

'Ten out of ten.'

She picked up my medical encyclopedia and began leafing through the section on First Aid. (Incidentally, have you ever wondered what happens if First Aid doesn't work? Is there any such thing as Second Aid or Third Aid, or do the doctors and nurses just give up? I mean, it's a bit worrying, isn't it?)

After a few pages she turned to me and

said it was little wonder I spent most of my time worrying. 'If you stopped reading stuff like this, you wouldn't fret so much.'

'I like reading that stuff. Listen, do you know what to do if a poisonous snake bites you?'

'No.'

'There you are then.'

'Rob, when did you last see any kind of snake round here?'

I couldn't answer that one. I was about to ask if she thought there was such a thing as Second Aid when Norman suddenly appeared outside his house. 'Quick! Look!' Bogbrush gazed out of the window. Her lips twisted into a curl.

'He is *weird*!' she said, and I could have hugged her. (I said I *could* have. I didn't say I did.) At last someone seemed to be thinking what I was thinking.

'And there's his mum,' I pointed out. 'Look, you can see part of the mark.'

'Spooky.' Bogbrush stared hard. 'I'd like to get a closer look at that. I should be able to recognize it. Anyhow, I thought you said their skin was yellow?'

'That's when they're in their alien state. At the moment they're pretending to be humans.'

'When do you think they'll be ETs then?'

'Tonight. I'm sure they slip into their alien condition at night.'

'What do you think we should do?' Bogbrush turned away from the window.

'I was hoping you'd have a plan.'

'Not really. I suppose the first thing to do is prove that they are aliens, and there's only one way to do that.' She sat down and fiddled with a pencil. 'We shall have to get into their house at night and take photos of them in their alien state. That will prove it to everyone.'

My heart had come to a complete stop. 'Into their house? Are you mad? We may as well ask them to kill us now.'

'Don't be so wet. It's not like we're going to knock on the door. We sneak in when they're asleep.'

This idea was pretty mind-blowing. I mean, normally when you make a new friend and ask them round to your house, you listen to music together or maybe play a game on the computer. Bogbrush was suggesting we sneak into somebody else's house in the middle of the night and take snapshots of them. It was fantastically exciting and horrifyingly scary . . . and it could just work. I nodded slowly.

'All right, we'll do it, as long as I have time to make my will before we go. Have you got a camera?'

'No.'

'Bogbrush! Why suggest it if you haven't got one?'

Bogbrush lifted her chin and those vague eyes of hers suddenly went into sharp focus. 'You call me Bogbrush and I'll call you Chicken Licken, OK? How do you want to play this, Rob?'

Talk about turning red! I felt like a nude beetroot. 'Sorry,' I muttered. 'I think my dad's got a camera downstairs. I'll see if I can find it.'

'How do we get into the house?'

I smiled. This was the easy bit. 'I've got a key. The last people who lived there gave my parents a spare key so that Mum could feed their cat when they went away. We've still got it, and I don't think the locks have been changed.'

Marsha and I looked at each other. This plan was suddenly becoming a very real thing. We were going to do it. We were going to enter the alien stronghold, and I hadn't even decided what I wanted written on my gravestone. My heart started fluttering again, like a little bird between a cat's jaws. 'OK,' I said, 'meet up by the bushes in our front garden at midnight, yeah?'

Marsha nodded. The colour had drained from her face. I asked her if she was scared and she shook her head, her tight curls bouncing about her face. 'No way!' she said quickly. At the door she turned back to me. 'I'm petrified,' she said, and vanished down the stairs.

I was astonished. I had never realized that Bogbrush – sorry, Marsha – had words like 'petrified' in her vocabulary. I had to go and look it up in the dictionary. She was turning out to be a dark horse. (Or a stone.)

I was left in my bedroom, thinking. Suddenly this whole business was turning into something real. I wasn't on my own any more, worrying about alien invaders. Marsha was with me, and we were really doing something. Scary stuff, eh?

5 What Kind of Cheese?

We never made it that night. We managed to meet up all right. Marsha was already waiting when I finally got outside. It had taken me longer than I thought to get ready. I kept forgetting things like my Swiss Army penknife, torch, compass, chocolate rations, signalling mirror, Dad's camera and so on. Then I had to go back for bandages and plasters, just in case, and finally I went back for the emergency foil blanket. (I had read somewhere that shiny foil can protect you from some alien weapons.) I stuffed everything into a rucksack.

'Where are you going?' hissed Marsha, staring at the rucksack. 'On safari?'

'You never know what you might need,' I explained. I felt a bit embarrassed, but I had to ask her. 'Are you wearing clean underwear?'

'None of your business!'

We stood there shivering in the shadows and we were just plucking up enough courage to cross the road when this UFO turned up. Well, I say 'turned up', but I suppose that sounds as if it came wandering over like some kid at a party with nobody to talk to. (I know how that feels!) It sounds silly, but that's how it was.

This UFO arrived from nowhere, silently, up in the sky, high above the Vorks' house. It was the faintly shimmering lights that first caught our attention. They rippled round its edges. In the darkness of the night sky it was difficult to make out its shape properly, but it appeared to be flat and circular, and there seemed to be a hole in the centre of the base. It stayed in the same place, hovering at high altitude, and it was all so strange. The sky was clear and full of stars, like any other night on Earth, and here, bang in the middle of it, was a craft from another world.

And then the colours came. They came in transparent waves, like drifts of coloured gauze: yellow, green and blue, radiating out from beneath the craft, spreading and sinking towards the ground, right behind the Vorks' house. There was no noise, just the lights, and then they stopped and the UFO drifted away into the night. I was rooted to the spot.

'Did you see that?'

'Fabulous!' said Marsha, with a rapturous smile.

'How can you say that?'

'I can hardly believe it. I've seen a real UFO!'

'We have to tell someone. This is getting far too dangerous. We can't handle this by ourselves. We must go to the police.'

Marsha swung her torch on to my face, almost blinding me. 'What do you think they'll do? Chase it with a squad car? Arrest it for parking in mid-air?' She began to laugh. 'This road hasn't even got double yellow lines. Anyhow, it's gone.'

'We have to do something,' I insisted.

'Tell your parents then.'

'Oh come on! If they know I've been out here at this time of night . . .'

Marsha nodded. 'I know what you mean. It's funny, isn't it? We could be out here saving the world and all my mum would say would be "Never mind the alien invasion – you get back to bed at once!" Crazy.'

'Snap.'

We gazed at each other for several seconds and then decided. 'Police!' we chorused, and set off for the police station, running like the wind. Well, I ran like the wind – Marsha ran more like a drunken giraffe. She tripped over her legs at least once on the way.

I guess we realized it was a mistake the moment we opened our mouths and said 'aliens' to the desk-sergeant. He began asking why we were out at that time of night, did our parents know, etc., etc. I mean, police are just like parents in uniform really, aren't they?

'And what did this UFO look like?' asked the desk-sergeant, grinning at all his mates who had turned up to have a laugh at our expense. I struggled for words.

'It was dark,' I began.

'Yes, a common phenomenon at night-time,' said the sergeant.

'He meant the UFO was dark,' scowled Marsha. 'It was a hazy shape, shadowy.'

I nodded. I could almost hear my English teacher hammering on about using similes to explain things more clearly.

'It was like a giant, circular cheese-box,' I said. 'You know, the ones with little foil triangles inside.'

The sergeant clicked his tongue several times and tapped his pencil on the desk. 'So, let's see if I've got this down correctly. There was this giant, round camembert floating through the sky . . .'

'I didn't say it *was* a cheese,' I pointed out acidly.

'*Like* a cheese-box,' Marsha reminded him. 'And it was too.'

A stout policeman in his shirt-sleeves came and stood by the sergeant. He fixed us with a serious frown. 'Are you sure it was a camembert? It could have been gorgonzola . . .'

'. . . or cheddar,' suggested a young

constable, but the sergeant shook his head.

'No, no, wouldn't have been cheddar. That's more sort of wedge-shaped.'

Honestly, this attempt at humour was at my dad's level. 'You don't believe us, do you?' I asked.

'No, we don't.'

'And you're not even going to ask around to see if anyone else saw what we saw?'

'No. But I'll tell you what I am going to do.'

'Telephone our parents,' sighed Marsha.

The young constable grinned. 'She can read your thoughts, sir! Spooky-doos!'

Ten minutes later our parents turned up, all three of them. I hadn't realized that Marsha lived with her mum. Her dad was somewhere else. (I'll tell you later. Don't rush me.)

So, imagine the little scene that now followed. Imagine *your* parents turning up at a police station in the middle of the night to collect you. All this time they thought you were safe and sound in bed, fast asleep, and now they discover that you've been roaming the streets after midnight . . . with a girl.

You know those English exercises you do at school sometimes, where you have to choose the right word to complete the sentence? Well try this one:

Your parents discover that you have been roaming the streets, after midnight, in the company of a girl. Are they angry, furious, ballistic, raging, explosive, going nuclear, volcanic, delighted, happy, cheerful, laughing?

I guess you would probably choose the same as me. Every one of those words except the last four.

However, that only describes my very predictable parents. What I found odd, as I was being dragged away to my hundred-year jail sentence at home, was Marsha's mum. She didn't seem surprised at all. She sort of sighed and apologized to the police for wasting their time. She gave me a strange look and asked Marsha if she'd been out star-gazing again. Marsha nodded and winked across at me.

That was the last I saw of her that night. In the car going home I was subjected to the kind of questioning that spies are put through in order to extract top-secret information from them, and then finally Mum and Dad got on to the big stuff.

'This has to stop, Robert.'

'There was a UFO,' I insisted. 'The Vorks are aliens.'

'Stop it at once! You are living in a fantasy world. You spend far too much time worrying about things that can never happen.'

'I only . . .'

'Not another word. That's enough. We're fed up to the back teeth with all this. Go to bed and stay there!'

I went up to my room and stood at the window, gazing across the street. OK, Vorks, I thought. You win for the time being, but I'm coming back and I won't be alone. I shall have Marsha with me.

Somehow I didn't think the aliens would be terribly scared, but I went to bed feeling a bit better.

6 Serious Stuff

Today's horoscope: You make a discovery that could change everything. Romance is in the air. Watch out for that new person in your life.

You probably want to know what happened to Marsha's father. At lunchtime the next day, at school, Marsha told me that he had fallen in love with another woman. 'Now they're living with each other. He left two years ago.'

I was a bit shocked. To tell you the truth I didn't really know what to say next, and when I did, I wished I'd kept my mouth shut. 'That is gross.'

Marsha snorted back at me. 'Grow up, Rob.'

This remark made me feel small and pathetic, and I don't mean in the cuddly hamster kind of way. I mean that snapped rubber band feeling, and a manky wet rubber band at that. I couldn't understand how Marsha could be so cool about such a thing.

'I'm sorry,' I offered.

'That's exactly what Dad said when he left,' Marsha answered in a tight voice.

'Do you miss him?' She nodded and I said brightly that she could have my dad if she wanted.

'Don't joke about it, Rob. You'd miss him if he wasn't there, I'm telling you.' Marsha gave me a twisted kind of smile. 'You don't want to, but you do.'

This was getting embarrassingly heavy for me and I desperately tried to change the subject. 'Why did your mum ask you if you'd been star-gazing again?'

'It's my hobby, astronomy.' Everything began to click into place, how Marsha had known about distant galaxies and all that stuff. 'I go out sometimes with the telescope Dad gave me last year. I have to go out at night. You can't see stars by day.'

'I do know that.'

'Of course you do, only my mum doesn't. She doesn't like me going out when it's dark.'

I was struck by a thought. 'Maybe she doesn't like it because you're using the telescope your dad gave you.'

Marsha gave me a sharp look. 'Never thought of that. Quite a little psychologist, aren't you? I suppose you read about it in your medical encyclopedia?' She saw the look on my face, apologized and began to laugh.

'What?'

'It's just that in the last five minutes we've both had to say sorry to each other.'

We were silent for a while, until I eventually plucked up enough courage to ask Marsha why she let people at school call her Bogbrush. 'You don't like me doing it.'

'*You* should know better. Anyhow, I don't care about them. I don't need them as friends. They don't bother me. When I want a friend I'll find someone I actually like, and it will probably be someone who doesn't care what small-minded people think about them, somebody who's just his own self.'

'Everybody is his own self!'

Marsha shook her head. 'No way. Most people go around trying to be the person they think others want them to be.'

Wow! I mean, what do you say when someone comes up with something like that? It took me almost five minutes just to work out what she meant. It was no wonder everyone kept clear of Marsha. Just listening to her talking made me want to go 'Ah! Stop it! My brain's hurting! It's turning to jelly!' So I did.

'You're making my brain turn to jelly.'

'It's called thinking, Rob,' Marsha declared. 'It's just that your brain's not used to it.'

'Thanks a lot.'

'Sorry. You're better than the others at school, but you could try using your brain a bit more, you know.'

'It's OK for you,' I whined. 'It doesn't hurt your brain.'

'You don't know that.'

I thought, *Here we go again. She's got an*

answer for everything. Quick, time to change the subject. (This is basically my trick for getting out of anything that seems to be going the wrong way – change the subject.)

'What are we going to do about the Vorks?' I asked in desperation.

Marsha folded her arms and smiled at me. 'That's typical,' she murmured, 'trying to change the subject.' So now Marsha was reading my thoughts too! She gave a long sigh. 'All right, I guess we shall have to try and get in there again. Without proof, nobody will listen to us.'

'Tonight?' I suggested, and she nodded. 'We'd better make it later than last night then. My parents will be on double alert.'

'I doubt that. They'll never think you'll be stupid enough to try it two nights in succession. Tonight will be ideal.'

'I hope you're right. What about two o'clock?'

'OK. I'd better go. If people see us talking like this they'll start thinking stupid things.'

'I thought that sort of thing didn't bother you?' I said.

'I was thinking of you,' Marsha snapped

back and she strode off, this time without
tripping over herself.

That evening I sat upstairs and re-read my
horoscope.

*You make a discovery that could change
everything.*

That could only mean what was going to
happen tonight. Tonight was the night! We
were really going to see the aliens!

*Romance is in the air. Watch out for that new
person in your life.*

Uh-oh. I didn't want to know about this.
'I'm too young for romance,' I said and was
startled to hear Mum the other side of my
bedroom door.

'Are you talking to yourself in there,
Robert?'

'It was the aliens,' I grunted.

Mum opened the door and put her head
round the corner. 'Don't be cheeky. I told
you, not another word about aliens. Poor
Marsha's mother. Heaven alone knows what

she thought about last night. Who is that girl anyway? She seemed ever so strange.'

Mum thinks most people are strange for one reason or another. She'll say things like, 'Look at that man. Isn't he strange?' or 'What a strange woman!' Then you look at the people she's looking at and there's nothing strange about them at all. What *is* strange is that you can put a couple of aliens right in front of Mum and she doesn't even notice.

'Her name's Marsha. She's in my class. She's clever.'

'She didn't look clever, and it certainly was not at all clever to go gallivanting round the streets at midnight.' She paused and then asked, oh so casually, 'Is she your girlfriend?'

'Mum, that is so predictable.'

'Ooh! That's a big word, Robert.'

'It was in our spelling test last week,' I muttered. 'Can I get on with what I was doing now?'

'What was that?'

'Thinking.'

Mum widened her eyes and tiptoed

theatrically from the room so as not to disturb the Great Thinker. She didn't know that I was actually thinking about Marsha, or, to be more precise, about Marsha and her parents. I tried to imagine what it would be like not having a dad and I just couldn't. It was too difficult.

Then I began worrying. Suppose *my* dad went off? Or Mum? I would probably be the last to know. I remembered the times they quarrelled, the times they hardly spoke to each other.

Maybe this was what my horoscope meant. This was the discovery that could change my life! Maybe the romance was not about me at all, but about *one of my parents*! Maybe the new person in my life was going to be a stepfather or stepmother.

NO! This was all going horribly wrong! I jumped to my feet and pounded downstairs. Mum was just sitting down in front of the television. I swallowed hard. 'Can I ask you something?'

'Of course.'

'You won't be cross, or laugh at me or anything?'

Mum shook her head. Any other mother would probably have said, 'I can see there's something worrying you, son,' but Mum knew that I was always worried anyway. She kept quiet and waited for me to speak. You know what I wanted to ask? I wanted to say, 'Do you still like Dad? Are you thinking of leaving?' But I knew it was stupid. I couldn't ask her questions like that. I tried to think of some other way of putting it, but nothing seemed right.

'It doesn't matter,' I said.

'Was it about Marsha?' Mum prompted, with a tiny, knowing smile she thought I wouldn't notice. Parents, eh? What do you do with them? You can read them like a book.

7 Diddle-iddle-dang Time

At 2 a.m., I met Marsha behind the bushes in our front garden. The first thing I did was ask her how you could tell if your mum or dad was about to leave.

'Don't be stupid, Rob. I don't know how you manage to cope with the inside of your head. It must be dreadful, worrying all the time about absolutely everything and nothing at all.'

'What do you mean?'

'Take a look at yourself. You've got that ridiculous rucksack with you again, stuffed full of rubbish I bet, just in case. Anyway, your parents are fine.'

'But they quarrel. They don't speak to

each other sometimes and . . .'

'Everyone is like that. Look at us. We quarrel too.'

'We're not married,' I pointed out.

Marsha laughed. 'Stop fretting and try relaxing a bit more.'

'Yeah, well, it's a bit difficult to relax when you live opposite a house stuffed with aliens.' I stared across at the dark building opposite. The street was still and silent. The only light came from the orange street lamps. Further up the road a cat trotted from one side to the other, then back again and then crossed a third time.

'Why doesn't that cat make up its mind?' I wondered out loud, but I knew how it felt.

'Are you ready?' Marsha asked, sounding a touch nervous herself.

We slipped out of the garden and ran quickly across the road, up the Vorks' front path and over to the front door. Marsha crouched down, putting her ear to the letterbox and listening for several seconds.

'Not a sound,' she whispered, and nodded to me. I slid the spare key into the lock and a moment later we were inside. I gently closed the door behind us and leaned back against it, breathing fast.

I felt dreadful. My heart was banging away all over the place, like a tumble-dryer that had broken free from its moorings. (I hope my English teacher sees this.) I knew people could die of fright, and now it was happening to me. I breathed hard and clamped both hands over my chest to stop my heart banging its way out through my ribcage.

'I think I'm having a heart attack,' I told Marsha.

'Don't be stupid,' she scowled. 'I'm scared too.'

'Who said I was scared?' I squeaked. 'I said I was having a heart attack. I mean, don't worry *too* much, will you?'

Marsha was standing in the dark shadow of the hall, but I could see the whites of her eyes glinting at me. 'If you're having a heart attack then you'd better go home and have a lie-down, hadn't you?'

I dropped my hands from my chest. 'It's OK now,' I said, breathing more easily.

Marsha sort of chuckled and shook her head. 'What?' I asked. 'What now?'

'Doesn't matter, Rob. Come on.'

We moved up the hallway, ears on alert. For some strange reason there were two giant-sized fridge-freezers parked in the passage. We squeezed past them. Closed doors stood like sinister sentries on either side of us. Marsha pointed to the nearest one. She reached down and began to turn the handle, very, very slowly, screwing up her eyes anxiously. She edged the door open and we both stared into the room, trying to make out what was inside.

Nothing.

Well, no aliens at any rate, just loads of monitors and computers and top spec electronic equipment. The Vorks certainly liked their . . . *DINNGG!* The penny dropped into both our brains at the same time. This room was full of hi-tech stuff, I mean FULL of it. Nobody in their right mind would want so much of it. And it wasn't ordinary TVs, it was weird stuff – banks and banks of switches and dials, controls and knobs and buttons.

Little lights flashed and danced on some of the machines. There were tiny screens and one huge viewing monitor, hanging on the wall like a picture that had been stolen. (Yeah, yeah, OK, I know what you're thinking – how can a picture hang there if it's been stolen? I mean the picture itself wasn't there. It was like a silent, empty TV screen, only empty TV screens aren't menacing and this thing was, as if it was trying to tell us something horrible.) This room made the deck of the *Starship Enterprise* look like something from *Blue Peter*, and it was obviously some kind of control room.

We slipped out of the room and poked around in the kitchen and the back of the house, but there was nothing there. It was time to go upstairs.

You know those films where you just see someone's feet going up the shadowy stairs of a dark, dark house? There's really creepy music playing and every so often a stair gives a faint creak and the foot pauses for a moment and then goes on and up and the tension mounts and mounts until you realize you've chewed all your fingernails to bits and now you're starting on your knuckles and your eyes are bulging fit to burst and the blood is ringing in your ears and you're on hyper-alert . . .?

It was just like that. Marsha was ahead of me. My eyes were glued to her feet as she went up. Every little creak and she would freeze, listen and then move on once more and the spooky music in my head was getting louder and louder . . .

Dee-dmmm! Dee-dmmm! Diddle-iddle-iddle-iddle-iddle! Dang-dang-dang-dang!

'Rob!' Marsha suddenly hissed, making me jump.

'What?'

'Stop singing!'

'I wasn't singing!'

'You were. You were going "Diddle-iddle-dang" or something. Shut up!'

I clenched my lips shut and followed in silence. We reached the top without any trouble. I pointed to a door on the left which was slightly ajar. Marsha pushed it open.

The bathroom. Nothing strange there. We moved down to the next door. For some reason I found myself wondering what I would say if we were caught. I tapped Marsha's shoulder and she silently mouthed back at me, 'What?'

'Let's say we're sleepwalking,' I whispered.

'What are you going on about now?'

'If we're caught, we can say that we're sleepwalking.' I nodded at her frantically. It seemed a good idea to me, but Marsha didn't look very impressed.

'What? Both of us? We both end up sleepwalking in the same house, in the same room, on the same night? Do you really think super-intelligent aliens are going to believe that?'

'They might. Anyhow, have you got a better idea?'

'Yes. If they wake up we run for our lives, OK?'

'It's not very sophisticated,' I grunted. (That was in last week's spelling test too.)

The handle squeaked as Marsha carefully turned it. She edged the door open and there they were, and I mean –

THERE THEY WERE!!!

Four aliens, lined up like bugs in a rug.

They seemed to hang there in the gloom: still, silent and fast asleep. Even in the darkness we could make out their sallow skin. It looked smooth, shiny and hard. A faint, flickering glow surrounded each body like an aura.

The bodies themselves were shaped like large jars, with broad shoulders that tapered down to a point at the bottom, like a wasp's sting. They each had three, very thin legs. There didn't seem to be any kind of head, but tentacles sprouted from the open neck, at least ten to each alien. The tentacles were as long as their bodies and from time to time they moved slightly. I could see they were covered with a spiralling line of frills, running from shoulder to tip. Something about those frills made me think – poison!

How long Marsha and I stood there gazing at these monsters I don't know. All I could think was, these creatures really are aliens. There are aliens in the house across the road. ALIENS!

Marsha nudged me and mimed taking the photograph. I nodded and slipped the rucksack from my shoulder. I undid the top and searched for the camera. I pulled out the spare torch and placed it quietly on the floor. I got out several boxes of plasters, toe-nail clippers, a sling for a broken arm and a thermometer.

'We want to take their photograph,' hissed Marsha. 'Not their temperature! Hurry up!'

I rummaged inside the bag again, found a road-map of Europe and put it on the floor.

'What's that for!'

'In case we get lost.'

'We're in the house across the road. How can we get lost?'

'Suppose they kidnap us and take us away in their spaceship?'

'A map of Europe won't be much use, will it?' growled Marsha. Maybe she was right, but I still found it comforting.

At last I located the camera and lifted it quietly from the rucksack. Marsha scowled, but gave me a thumbs-up sign. I removed the lens cap, got all four aliens lined up in the viewfinder, and then had an awful thought.

'What happens if the flash wakes them up?'

'I told you, run for it.'

I swallowed nervously. 'Can we stand nearer the door then?' Marsha moved towards the door and I followed. I put the viewfinder to my eye once more, took a deep breath and pressed the button.

Nothing happened. For several seconds Marsha and I stood there, frozen with tension. Then I tried again, but still nothing happened. I shook the camera and peered at it in confusion.

'Why doesn't it work?' she asked.

I lowered the camera slowly and looked up into Marsha's face. 'It hasn't got any film in it,' I said.

'*Rob!!*'

Instantly a loud humming filled the room, like a gigantic swarm of killer bees stirring into life. The long tentacles began to rustle, their tiny frills sniffing and feeling the air.

'Run for it!' yelled Marsha, and we practically fell down the stairs and went shooting out of that house like bullets from a gun. We raced down the road, round the

corner, along the next street, round another
corner and had almost reached the town
centre before we slowed down and stopped.
We collapsed panting in the dark doorway
of a shop.

'It's OK,' Marsha croaked, looking back
down the road. 'There's no sign of them.'

I leaned back against the door, feeling its
solid, cold hardness press into my back. It
was very reassuring. 'What do we do now?' I
asked.

'I don't know.'

'Those were real aliens, Marsha.'

'I know.'

'From outer space.'

'Yeah.'

'I mean, they *were* – real aliens!'

'I know. Stop going on.'

'We've got to do something,' I whined.
Marsha shuffled her long legs anxiously.

'Police? I don't think so,' she said. 'Not
after last time. They'll just ring our parents
again and this time we shall really be in
trouble.' We were both beginning to calm
down a bit – not a lot – but I reckon my
heart had slowed from about three thousand

beats per second to a mere three hundred. It even felt as if it was back in the right place behind my ribs and not slopping about round my ankles as if my trousers had fallen down.

'They don't know it was us,' Marsha pointed out. 'I'm sure they didn't see us. We leave everything for tonight, but tomorrow you put some film in that camera, we go back and get that photograph.'

'But they'll be suspicious.'

'Stop worrying, Rob. They'll just think it was a cat or something.'

'Really?' Marsha didn't sound very convincing. We slipped back to our homes.

The next day was a Saturday, so I was able to sleep in a bit. Even so, Mum had difficulty in waking me I was so exhausted. She kept shaking me.

'Rob? Rob! Wake up now! Norman's come to see you.'

I sat up with a jerk. Norman? Alarm bells began to go off in my head and I rubbed my eyes. Norman Vork?

At that moment he appeared in the doorway of my bedroom, one hand behind his back. He gazed across at me with a horrible smirk and then lifted his arm.

'I think this rucksack is yours,' he said.

8 Walking on Tentacles

Today's horoscope: Be careful in open spaces. Stay indoors if you can.
Small animals could bring you great fortune.

I shook my head. 'No, no, no way. It's not mine.'

'Yes it is,' said Mum, ever helpful. 'We gave that to you last Christmas.'

'It looks like mine, but it's not mine,' I insisted.

'It's got your name inside,' Norman snarled, and even Mum took a step back.

'Oh, *that* rucksack!'

Norman looked across at my mother. He didn't speak, he just stared at her. I was astonished to see her turn red. She gave him a faint smile. 'I'll be downstairs then,' she said, and went. Truly spooky! It was as if he'd silently ordered her to go, moulded her thoughts somehow.

Norman sat himself on the edge of my bed. I pulled the duvet up to my chin. 'So,' he hissed, and his eyes bored into mine. 'How much do you know?'

'What about?' I stalled. Norman folded his arms and gazed at me steadily. It might have been my imagination, but I reckoned I could see little red dots coming out of his eyes . . . doot-doot-doot-doot-doot. I think he was trying to hypnotize me, just like he had my mother, so I looked at the duvet cover instead. It was the one with Thomas the Tank Engine all over it.

Yeah, yeah, I know what you're thinking, Thomas the Tank Engine! What a baby! Listen, when I was five I thought Thomas the Tank Engine was wonderful. But now I felt ridiculously embarrassed. I mean, here I was, talking to a dangerous alien, with nothing between us except my Thomas the Tank Engine duvet cover.

'My parents gave me this when I was little,' I explained nervously. 'I don't like him any more.'

All at once Norman leaned forward and pushed his face close to mine. 'You were in our house last night. We know. It's no good pretending, Rob. I can read your thoughts.'

'Really? What am I thinking then?' and I shut my eyes and tried hard to think of something which had nothing to do with aliens at all.

Norman laughed. 'You're wishing you didn't feel so scared.'

Now it was my turn to go red. He was dead right. But I suddenly thought, if Norman knows what I'm thinking, then why pretend? Just tell him everything. So I did.

'I know all about you and your family,' I muttered through gritted teeth. (I had to grit them together to stop them clattering with fear.) Norman tried to appear ultra-cool and sneered back at me.

'Oh yeah? Such as?'

'I know you and your family are creatures from another galaxy, and I know you've come to take over the world.'

Boy, you should have seen his face. Talk about surprised! His jaw really did drop, and he stared at me, flabbergasted. He couldn't speak for several moments, and when he did it was to ask me a question.

'Do I look like an alien? Do any of my family look like aliens?'

'Of course not. It's daylight.'

'It's daylight,' repeated Norman, keeping his eye fixed on mine.

'It's only at night that you take on your true form. I know that. That's why I was in your house last night. I was going to photograph you all in your real monster state.'

For several more moments Norman just gazed at me, a little frown on his forehead. Slowly, a smile began to creep on to his face. It wasn't a nice smile.

'You were very lucky, Chicken Licken,' he began. 'We hadn't finished the shield last night. If we had, you'd be dead.'

'Really?' I tried to sound OK about this news, but my voice came out all squeaky. My voice is always letting me down like that. 'What's the shield?'

'It's an invisible defence wall we throw round our craft, or wherever we happen to be. It's made from photonic particles. Our enemies just walk into it and pzzzz! That's it, like those electric fly-traps. It just makes a tiny noise. Nobody would hear, nobody would know. Pzzzz – and you're zapped, gone up in smoke, nothing left, except maybe your socks and shoes.'

And you know, the stupid thing is, despite being terrified at my near brush with death, what I was actually thinking was, Only my shoes and socks left, so it wouldn't matter if I wasn't wearing clean underpants.

'Of course, nobody will believe you if you tell them we're aliens.' Norman looked very pleased with himself. 'You humans are so stupid. Especially you.' He laughed and then asked how I'd got into his house.

'You know everything,' I said. 'You tell me.'

'You didn't break in,' said Norman.

'No, I didn't.' I was secretly very pleased that Norman didn't know that there had been two of us in the house. I had to keep Marsha up my sleeve. (Just a figure of speech; she wouldn't actually fit up there of course, unless they were super-baggy sleeves, and extra long. Even then she'd probably fall out. She's always falling somewhere.)

'So you had a key. Where is it?'

I reached down and got it from my trouser pocket. I handed it over. Norman at last got off the bed and stood up.

'Tell as many people as you like,' he growled. 'But don't come near our house. From now on the shield will be in force. Our people are coming, Rob, and nobody can stop them. Keep out of trouble and you won't get hurt. Come anywhere near us again and . . .' Norman broke off and grinned. His face was pure Evil. He dropped the rucksack on to my lap. 'I think you'll find some bandages in there,' he said. 'You come anywhere near us and you'll need them.' And he went.

I have never got dressed so fast in all my life. My thoughts were whirling round my brain like some de-railed helter-skelter car. I had to do something. I had to tell someone, but every thought I came up with was a dead end. Mum and Dad? No. Police? No. Army? How do you ring the army anyhow? I mean, I don't suppose they're in the Yellow Pages. The only person I could think of was Marsha. I raced round to her house.

Her mum was pretty surprised to see me, but at least she gave me a smile. 'Marsha's still asleep,' she explained.

'Wake her up,' I said.

'I beg your pardon?'

I jiggled up and down on the doorstep. 'Sorry, I mean, please wake her up, Mrs Zewlinsky. It's very, very important.'

Marsha's mum gave me another little smile and sighed. 'Come on in. Sit down over there and I'll see if I can get her up, but don't expect any miracles. She's like a bear with a sore head most mornings.' Marsha's mum disappeared and several moments later I heard raised voices, then her mum came back down. 'Bear with a sore head,' she repeated, adding 'Rather you than me,' before disappearing off into the little garden out the back.

Marsha herself appeared in the doorway. She was in her pyjamas and dressing gown, her hair all dishevelled. (Not that it made much difference: her hair was always dishevelled.) 'Oh,' she groaned. 'It's you.'

I leaped to my feet. 'They know,' I said. 'Norman's been to see me. He brought my rucksack back.'

'You never left it behind?'

I nodded sheepishly and Marsha gave a long, long sigh while I wildly babbled on about invasions and preparations and everything. 'He admitted everything. And he said it's too late to do anything,' I shouted at her, 'but we've got to do *something*.'

Marsha sat down on the edge of the settee. 'It could be true then,' she murmured, and then gave me a cross glance. 'Just calm down, will you?'

'But they're going to invade!'

Marsha leaned across and gripped both my wrists to stop them shaking. She stared at me fiercely and said, 'Do you want me to call you Chicken Licken?'

I took a deep breath, held it and then let it out slowly. 'OK, I'll stop panicking, but we must do something.'

'First we must think. They're making preparations, you say? What sort of preparations? What do we know about them? Norman told you his dad was a computer whizz, right? So my guess is that they are going to hack into our defence systems, worldwide.'

'Can that be done?'

'Probably. They bring down the defence systems and that means any invading force can just walk in.'

'They've got tentacles,' I pointed out. 'I don't think it's possible to walk on tentacles. You have to sort of, well, slip and slop I suppose.'

'Rob, it doesn't matter how they get here. We must stop them, remember?'

'We have to warn people,' I said.

'And to do that we must have proof that they are ETs. We've got to actually show the police or the army or whoever some real aliens – what we saw for ourselves last night.'

'We can't go back and photograph them,'

I protested. 'Not now,' and I told Marsha about the shield. 'We have to move fast,' I went on.

And then it happened. You know how sometimes you get an idea that is so fantastic and simple you just can't believe how clever you really are? That's what happened to me. This idea suddenly made me realize what a brain was for. I mean, you could really *think* things! Really clever stuff! I grabbed Marsha's arm.

'We kidnap Norman.'

'Then what? Tell the entire ET invasion force that they must stop invading Earth or they won't get Norman back? Do you think evil aliens will let the life of one teenager stop them?' Marsha was scathing, but I didn't care. For once she hadn't realized what I meant.

'Have you finished?' I asked. 'That's not the idea at all. What happens to Norman and his family at night?'

'They turn into space monsters.'

'Exactly. We kidnap Norman. We keep him hidden until night-time. He turns back into an alien. Then we can show everyone and they will have to believe us.'

Marsha thought this over. 'Yeah. Actually, that's a pretty good idea, Rob. You're not as stupid as you look.'

'Neither are you,' I grinned. 'Come on, let's do it.'

'Do you think I could get out of my pyjamas first?' Marsha vanished upstairs and a little later her mother came in from the garden.

'So,' she smiled. 'You and Marsha are friends?'

'I suppose you could say that, yep.'

Marsha's mum watched me for several moments. 'I'm glad,' she said at last. 'Marsha doesn't have many friends.'

'I know. Everyone thinks she's weird.' I could have bitten my tongue right off at that moment. Me and my big mouth. Her mother laughed, just like Marsha's laugh, a throaty chuckle.

'She is a bit odd, but you know what people say – takes one to know one.' Marsha's mother gave me another smile and went back outside, leaving me to puzzle out what she had meant.

There was an almighty rumble and crash

as Marsha clattered down the stairs, tripped over her gangly legs and crashed in a heap on the hall floor. 'I'm all right!' she cried, beckoning wildly to me and we quickly left the house.

Our mission – to kidnap the alien known as Norman and keep him prisoner until nightfall.

9 Early Darkness

'Right,' said Marsha, as we hurried back to my house. 'How exactly are we going to kidnap Norman?'

'Chloroform,' I said at once. 'It's a chemical. You sprinkle it on a hanky and hold it over the person's nose and it makes them go unconscious.'

'And you've got some, have you?'

'Of course not! You can't just go out and buy it like sweets or something.'

'Why mention it then?'

'Because, if we *did* have it, it would be ideal.'

'Let's stick to the real world, shall we?' growled Marsha. 'What we need to do is keep hold of Norman somewhere safe until it gets dark.'

That was when I got my second brilliant idea. 'We could make the dark come early,' I said.

'What's that supposed to mean?'

'Norman turns into an alien when it gets dark, right? Why should we wait until it's night-time? Suppose we make it dark early — put him in a dark place? Then he'd turn into an alien straight away.'

Marsha stopped and stared at me. 'That's very good, Rob. Why aren't you like this in school? That's two excellent ideas you've had in ten minutes. A world record, I shouldn't wonder.' Marsha beamed at me. 'We could get a cardboard box and just pop it over Norman's head.'

'He's bound to struggle,' I pointed out, and I had this vision of Norman's fists flying about like manic sledgehammers. I didn't want to lose all my teeth.

'All right, we use a blanket instead and then we can pin down his arms at the same time.'

I wasn't so sure about this. Norman might

have been a bit thin and weedy, but he was still bigger and older than us. He wasn't likely to let us put a blanket over his head without fighting back. I automatically covered my teeth with one hand. 'Suppose he hits us?'

'We are trying to prevent space monsters taking over Earth, Rob. Somewhere along the line we might get injured. It's a risk we have to take.'

My stomach was churning up. I couldn't believe that Marsha could be so brave about the idea of being hurt. I mean, we were talking about teeth here, noses, real blood . . . maybe even DEATH. On the other hand, I couldn't bear to tell her that my stomach had turned into scarified jelly, not when she was being all calm and heroic about it.

We got to my house and found an old blanket. Our plan of action was simple. We would hide behind the hedge at the front of our house and wait until Norman walked past. Then we'd jump on him with the blanket. Simple ideas are always the best.

The hedge was tall, and we flattened

ourselves against its stiff branches, trying to make ourselves invisible. It was a pity it was a hawthorn hedge. 'Ow!'

'Shut up,' hissed Marsha.

'I've got a thorn in my bum!' I snapped back, and she sniggered.

'You always were a bit of a pain.'

'Thank you for your kind sympathy. You can get tetanus from things like this. It says so in . . .'

'. . . your medical encyclopedia,' Marsha finished wearily.

'And gangrene,' I added. 'Your skin puffs up and goes purple and black and green and it starts festering and eventually it just drops off.'

'Rob! You've only been pricked by a little thorn. Your bum's not going to fall off.'

'Says you. You'll be sorry if it does.'

'Not as sorry as you. You'll be bottom-less.' Marsha found this *so* amusing and began giggling again. 'You'll have to carry a bag with you, a bumbag, just in case, and a little shovel. Then when it happens, you can scoop it off the floor, bag it up and take it home. Maybe your mum can sew it back on or something.' By this time Marsha was in stitches.

'You're enjoying this, aren't you?' I grunted, rubbing my backside. 'It hurt.'

'Ssssh!' hissed Marsha. 'He's coming out! He's crossed the road.'

My heart immediately began banging about like a hyperactive drum kit. My fingers were gripping the blanket so hard my knuckles had gone white. Time seemed to stand still. The distant footsteps came closer and then stopped. 'What's he doing?' I panicked.

'Ssssh, just wait a sec. It's OK, he's coming.'

Norman's footsteps drew closer and closer. Then, through the tangle of twigs and leaves of the hedge we could see his shape as he began to pass by.

'Now!' cried Marsha. We leaped up and plunged out from behind the hedge, holding the stretched blanket in front of us. It worked like a dream. In a trice we had the blanket over his head and all three of us fell to the pavement, where we rolled about, pinning Norman's arms to his sides. He was snarling dreadfully under the blanket and thrashing his head from side to side. Marsha clung to it as if it were a rogue rugby ball. She shouted at me.

'Is he changing yet? Is he beginning to change?'

That was when the dream turned into a nightmare. I glanced at Norman's legs, and even though they were waggling about wildly in mid-air, *I could see at once that his legs had definitely changed.*

Norman the Alien was wearing lady's shoes, black tights and, well, I daren't mention anything else. (It wasn't my fault. You do see quite a lot when someone waves their legs about as much as that.)

'He's a woman!' I shouted at Marsha, who was still attempting touchdown with Norman's head. Marsha took one look and yelled. 'We've got the wrong person! Run for it!'

We took off like rabbits and didn't stop running until we reached the park. We threw ourselves panting on to the grass. At last we got our breath back.

'How did that happen?' I asked.

'I don't know. Norman must have stopped and gone somewhere else, and then some other person came along. Do you think she saw us? Who was it anyway?'

'I haven't a clue. I only saw her legs and . . .' I went pink '. . . not much else. Do you think it's safe to go back?'

We walked back to find a knot of chattering people gathered near our house, and a police car. We watched and waited, but nobody went up my front path so we guessed that nobody knew it had been us. We decided it was safe to get a bit closer.

'Someone tried to mug me,' said a loud voice, 'but I fought them off.' We peered through the crowd, and there was Mrs Parsloe, our next door neighbour-but-one, looking rather flustered and with her hair all messed up. (I wonder how that happened!) 'I gave him a black eye,' Mrs Parsloe declared. Marsha and I looked at each other and shook our heads in disbelief. The lying toad!

Anyhow, we decided the blanket was not such a good idea after all. Besides, Marsha had already come up with a much better plan. Apparently there was a cellar in her house which was only used for storing junk. Marsha said it was *very* dark down there. We sat up in my bedroom and discussed Plan Two.

'If we can lure Norman over to my house and get him in the cellar, that will be it. He'll be trapped. The only way out is through the door, and we can lock that. We wait for him to alter into his true form and then call the police.'

'It's a pity you didn't think of this before we tried the blanket,' I pointed out. A big smile took over Marsha's face and she gave that throaty chuckle.

'Yeah,' she said. 'That was really funny!'

I have to admit it is something I shall *never* forget. Mrs Parsloe's waggling legs were a pretty memorable sight. However, it was not going to save the world, so it was back to business.

'When do we try Plan Two?' I asked.

'Tomorrow afternoon. Mum's going out.

She's got a boyfriend. His name's Tony.'

This came as a bit of a shock, I can tell you. How could Marsha be so calm about it? 'Don't you mind?'

'Why should I?'

'I'd be really upset if my mum went out with a new boyfriend.'

'Your mum and dad haven't split up though, have they?'

'Not yet,' I said darkly.

'Don't start that again, Rob. Look, my mum's not going to sit around on her own for the rest of her life. Anyhow, it's none of your business.'

I shut up. Marsha was quiet for a few moments and then she went on. 'It could be a bit risky at my house. Mum might come back, but I can't think of anywhere else.'

Just then my own mum came back and called up the stairs. 'Are you in, Rob?'

'Upstairs. Marsha's here.'

'Oh.'

It's such a small word – 'oh'. You wouldn't think it could be said with such meaning. The way my mum said 'oh' actually meant, 'Well I never, upstairs with a girl, ho ho ho.' I ignored it. Marsha and I agreed that we would meet at her place the following afternoon and put Plan Two into action.

'Hello, Marsha,' Mum said cheerfully as I saw Marsha to the front door. 'You two seem to be very good friends these days?' Now Mum's face had a *ho ho ho* smile on it.

Marsha nodded seriously. 'Yes. We thought we'd get married tomorrow. See you, Rob.'

You should have seen Mum's face! She was left speechless. Her jaw had almost fallen off. I had to hand it to Marsha. Talk about sharp! I kept spilling my food at lunch I was laughing so much.

'It wasn't *that* funny, Rob,' Mum said crossly.

But it was.

10 Plan Two, with Several Emergency Measures

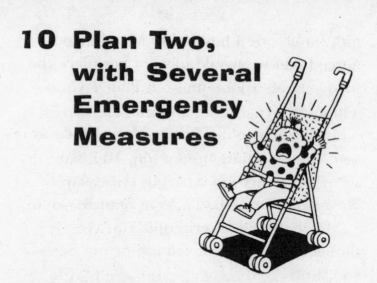

Today's horoscope: Avoid anything pink today. You will meet someone who will help you see things in a new light.

We had the house to ourselves. Marsha's mum had gone off to meet her boyfriend and now Marsha lay across an armchair, with her gangly legs dangling over one arm and her hands behind her head. How could she be so relaxed? I sat hunched on the edge of my seat, staring at the telephone.

'We ring Norman,' Marsha said. 'We tell him something that makes him come round here. Something that will also make him go down into the cellar.'

'Treasure. Tell him there's something valuable down there.'

Marsha shook her head and gazed at the ceiling. 'Norman's not a pirate. He's an extraterrestrial. Suppose we let him believe we know something about him. Tell him we've got something of his in our cellar?'

I was edgy. 'We've only got one chance to get this right. He won't fall for it twice. It's got to be good.'

'I know. We have to let him think we've got something important on him, but without telling him what.'

This was beginning to sound like complicated espionage stuff to me. 'You're going to make the call, aren't you?' I asked.

'Stop fretting and hand me the phone.' Marsha took several tissues and shoved them over the mouthpiece. A moment later she'd dialled and I'd turned into a nervous wreck. (Yes, again. Nervous wrecks are my speciality.) Marsha cleared her throat.

'NORMAN VORK?' Good grief! Marsha's voice had dropped two octaves. It even made me jump! It sounded as if she was talking from beyond the grave. 'We know all about *you*. We know what you're up to, you AND your family.' Marsha spoke slowly and deliberately. 'We have something of yours, something VERY important, something SECRET, something YOU wouldn't want anyone to know about. If you want us to keep quiet you'd better get over here fast, VERY fast, or we're going to the authorities, and you know what that means, Norman.'

Marsha spouted her address and put down the phone. She let out a long breath and collapsed back on the settee. She looked exhausted. Several minutes ticked by. I bit my lip.

'Do you think he'll come?'

'Definitely.' Marsha jumped up again and zipped into the cellar. 'I'm taking the bulb out so it's completely dark,' she called back. 'OK, are we ready? Rob, you look like a ghost. You're not going to faint on me, are you?'

Before I could answer, the doorbell rang. Through the frosted glass panel we could see a dark shape looming.

'It's him,' said Marsha, and I was glad to

see that even she looked a bit rattled. She took a deep breath and opened the door. Norman slunk in, scowling at the pair of us.

'You!' he sneered, as soon as he clapped eyes on me. 'I might have known. It's the Boy Who's Going to Save the World.' He turned on Marsha. 'So who are you then, the deputy sheriff?'

'You won't think you're so clever when you see what we've got,' Marsha said quietly, and she fixed him with one of her hooded glares.

'Oh yeah? Don't tell me, you've found one of our space ships in your back garden.'

'It's something a lot better than that,' said Marsha. 'It's down here. If you know what's good for you – and your family – you'd better take a look.' She stood to one side and showed him the open cellar door. Norman frowned, paused, and stepped inside.

BANG! The door slammed and I turned the key. In an instant Norman was hammering from the inside. 'Let me out, you slimy rats! Let me out of here!'

We listened to him for a moment and

watched the door quivering as he rained blows on the inside, but there was no way he could get out. We went back to the front room and sat down in triumph. We could still hear his shouts, but they were distant now, and after a while he stopped.

'He's probably starting to change,' I muttered. Marsha frowned.

'We have a small problem,' she began. 'I wish I'd thought of it before. We can't see if Norman's changed unless we open the cellar door. If we open the door he'll escape.'

A small problem? It seemed like a major catastrophe to me. What a situation to be in. We had to open the door to see, but we couldn't open the door or he'd escape. Marsha and I pondered our dilemma and a depressing silence began to fill the front room, a silence that was only broken by faint cries.

I sat up and listened. The whimpering seemed strange, as if someone really was crying. Was Norman sobbing in the cellar? Marsha had noticed too and we gazed at each other in puzzlement. I went to the door. The crying wasn't coming from the cellar. It was from beyond the front door.

We crept across the hall. There was definitely someone, or something, crying outside. Marsha whispered, 'I'll open the door and you rush out and surprise them.'

'How about I open the door and you rush out?' I suggested.

'We open the door and we both rush out,' Marsha said.

So we did. We dashed out and there was – a baby. Norman's little sister. Petal was sitting in her pushchair and crying and waving her little fists in the air.

'Her name's Petal,' I groaned, as Marsha pushed her inside. 'What do we do?'

'Why did Norman bring his little sister with him?' Marsha demanded crossly.

'I don't know. Ask him. Maybe he was looking after her when we rang and there was nobody at home to keep an eye on her, so he had to bring her.'

'Didn't you notice he had a baby with him when he arrived?' Marsha snapped.

'No. Did you?'

We stared at each other angrily. Marsha put her hands to her head and took several deep breaths. 'We'll have to take her back to their house.'

'That's crazy! The first thing the Vorks will do is ask us why we've got their baby. And suppose they're out?'

'We hand her in to the police then.'

'Are you mad? They'll ask us where we got her from. They'll ask hundreds of questions. They know us already, remember? "Was it a Camembert, or Gorgonzola?" You know what they're like.' Petal was still crying. 'Can't you stop her making that noise?'

'How am I supposed to do that?'

'You tell me. You're the girl.' Me and my big mouth! As soon as I said it, I wished the pavement would open up and swallow me whole.

Marsha stopped dead. 'What exactly do you mean by that, Rob? Are babies a girl-thing only? I don't think so. Are boys banned from looking after babies? I don't think so. Are boys unable to look after babies? I don't think so.' She glared at me. I was rapidly losing count of how many times Marsha glared at me these days. 'You're in this too, Rob. We are going to have to look after this baby, and I mean *we* – not me, by myself, on my own, without your help – but both of us, got it?' She paused, her nose wrinkled up and she added in a slightly scared kind of voice. 'They have nappies and . . . stuff.'

We both glanced at Petal. Nappies were definitely not top of my list of What to Do with a Yelling Baby.

'Maybe she's hungry,' I suggested.

'Maybe her nappy needs changing,' muttered Marsha.

'Let's try the easy end first,' I said, wheeling the pushchair into the kitchen. 'What do you think small space monsters eat?'

Marsha shook her head. 'Doesn't really matter, Rob, does it? I don't think Mum buys alien food very often. It's not the sort of thing we have much call for really.' Marsha had a point, I suppose. She opened the fridge and peered inside. 'She'll have to have cheese on toast. It's the only thing I know how to cook. Can't you stop her yelling? Pick her up or something.'

I stared at the screaming infant. Pick her up? Urgh! She might do something, like wee on me, or throw up. I've got an uncle and aunt with a little baby, and he's always doing stuff like that. I mean, he just LEAKS everywhere. I looked around for some kind of protection, but all I could find was a big, black bin-liner and some huge pink rubber kitchen gloves. I tore a hole in the bottom of the liner, one on each side, and pulled it over my head. I stuck my hands in the gloves.

Marsha fell about. 'What are you doing?'

I pulled the edges of the sack down around my legs and began unfastening Blubberbags from the pushchair. 'Listen, I am not going to have baby-sick all over my clothes, OK?'

'If you say so.' Marsha started cutting some slices of cheese, but she was still laughing. I could tell by the way her shoulders went up and down.

I tried calming the baby. I clutched her to my shoulder and bounced her up and down, but it didn't seem to make much difference. She carried on screaming into my left earhole until my brain began ringing. It was like having an entire ambulance station stuck inside your head.

I sat her back in the pushchair and tried to entertain her by pulling stupid faces. 'Look! Funny face!' I said. I went cross-eyed. I pulled out my ears. I made silly noises. I stuck out my tongue. That's when baby hit me. *BAMM!*

Boy, could she pack a punch! I crashed backwards and slammed against the open fridge. Half the contents came raining down on my head.

Have you ever noticed what people put in their fridges? I'll tell you – wet, cold things. Almost everything that goes into a fridge is wet, or cold, or both. My head was treated to a shampoo of milk, eggs, yoghurt, bacon slices, a piece of fish, fruit juice, tomatoes . . .

'Now look what you've done,' cried Marsha, 'and you were worried about the baby being sick. Rob, the entire fridge has just thrown up over you. Look at the mess you've made! Can't you do anything helpful?'

There was a muffled yell from the cellar. 'What's going on out there? Let me out!'

'Shut up!' I shouted back.

Then we realized that baby had stopped crying. Do you know what she was doing now? Laughing.

Laughing at ME.

You see? It's like I said, everyone does. How horrible can a baby get? First she smacks me in the face, and then she laughs at me. There is no justice.

11 We Find Out More About Babies

I set about cleaning myself up. At least the bin-liner had saved me from too much damage. Marsha finished off the cheese on toast and tried it out on Petal. Baby kept her mouth clamped shut. Marsha tried playing aeroplanes with her. You know, making the food fly through the air.

'Here it comes,' said Marsha, making her cheese-on-toast aeroplane dive out of the kitchen sky. 'Here it comes, nyeeeaaaaah, and open your mouth . . .' The mouth stayed shut and the cheese on toast almost crash-landed on Petal's face.

'I thought babies had to have their food all mashed up,' I said.

'Good idea.' Marsha got out an electric mixer. She put the toast in the bowl and switched on. Bits of toast and cheese disintegrated and went flying out of the bowl and all over the kitchen. Marsha switched off and surveyed the bits of brown and yellow stuck to the walls and ceiling. 'Maybe not such a good idea after all,' she murmured.

Petal didn't seem to think it was very funny either and started crying again. Marsha and I looked at each other. I knew what she was thinking. She knew what I was thinking. There was only one thing left to do. We would have to investigate The Other End.

'Bathroom,' said Marsha, and I agreed. Marsha grabbed Alien Monster and up we went. At this point I have to say I felt OK about the whole thing, because Marsha was holding the baby, and as long as I wasn't holding the baby, everything was all right. However, when we reached the bathroom Marsha suddenly handed baby over to me, while she ran the bath, and all at once I didn't feel OK at all.

'Don't make the water too hot,' I said. 'Babies are bathed in tepid water. You have to feel it with your elbow to make sure it's the right temperature.'

Marsha stared at me. 'How do you know?'

I smiled. 'It was in my medical encyclopedia, so there.' You know what? Marsha was actually impressed. She shoved her elbow into the bath, ran a bit more cold water and then began taking off baby's clothes. *Urgh!* It was like unwrapping a present you know you really don't want. This was a double first for me. Not only had I never changed a baby's nappy, I'd never seen alien poo before.

'Can you hold my nose for me?' asked Marsha in disgust, so I bent down and held her nose with one hand and my nose with the other. 'No wonder she was crying,' said Marsha, taking the nappy and sticking it into the bin. 'Right, you hold her steady while I wash her.'

It felt really weird. All that time I'd been thinking how horrible it would be, I mean looking after a baby and all that, but it

wasn't. In fact, I actually enjoyed it. It felt
. . . nice, cosy, fun. Petal kicked her little legs
and splashed us both. She gurgled and
giggled and blew bubbles. I glanced at
Marsha and noticed that her eyes had gone
soft and dopey.

She looked at me and grinned. 'Stop
looking so soppy, Rob.'

'She's going wrinkly round the edges,' I
snapped, fetching a towel. 'Dry her off.'

It was only after we'd dried baby that we
realized we didn't have a clean nappy for
her. 'Now what do we do?' I asked, and we
searched around for something, anything we
could use. All the bath towels were too big.

'We'll have to use loo roll,' said Marsha,
and that gave me an idea. I fished inside one
of my pockets and produced a roll of
bandage.

'How about this?'

'It's better than nothing, but how come
you've got something like this in your
pocket?'

'I always carry it, just in case.'

'Just in case what?'

I didn't dare tell Marsha how I lived in

fear of cutting myself badly, or breaking my arm or leg. 'In case I ever find a baby that needs an instant nappy,' I growled, and started winding the bandage round and round Petal's bottom. Marsha lifted her up.

'You'd better stop. She's beginning to look like an Ancient Egyptian mummy.'

We took Mini-monster downstairs and tucked her up on the sofa where, mercifully, she fell asleep. With her mouth and eyes shut at the same time she looked almost angelic. It was hard to believe that she was related to that dark and evil creature lurking in the cellar.

'Do you think Norman's changed yet?'

'Maybe. It probably takes a little while, like on the *X-Files*.'

I went out to the cellar door and listened. I kept expecting to hear alien noises, you know, hisses and slurps and growls, but there was nothing. Marsha seemed on edge.

'I just hope the others aren't able to track Norman and his sister to this house. They could try and get us.'

'We've got the baby,' I pointed out, and she nodded.

We stood and listened, but only silence drifted back, with just the occasional yell from Norman in the cellar. My eyelids drooped. I was worn out. Then we heard a key in the front door. It swung open and in walked Marsha's mother. We dashed into the hall.

'Oh, hello, Robert, you're here.' Mrs Zewlinsky gave me a second glance. 'You look in a bit of a mess. Everything all right?'

'Fine,' I said.

'It's just that you seem to have something stuck in your hair.' She looked more closely. 'A slice of tomato. How did that get there?'

Marsha and I suddenly remembered the kitchen. It still looked as if an elephant had had a birthday party in there. We had to keep Marsha's mum away. And out of the front room! I panicked. I tried desperately to think of some explanation for the mess, but Mrs Zewlinsky cut in on me.

'Would anyone like a drink?'

'No!' Marsha and I chorused and Marsha leaped towards the door.

'You can't be thirsty already, Mum,' she said.

Mrs Zewlinsky looked at both of us in turn. 'Is there something going on here? Anything I should know about?'

Marsha decided to tell the truth. Not all of it, but just a little bit. 'I made a bit of a mess in the kitchen, and we haven't cleaned up yet. Sorry, Mum.'

'We all make mistakes. At least you told me. Come on, I'll give you a hand.'

'I don't think you . . .' Marsha broke off. It was too late. Her mother was already in the kitchen.

Mrs Zewlinsky gazed at the walls and ceiling. She studied the floor in front of the fridge. 'You did say a bit of a mess?'

'A lot of a mess,' Marsha corrected herself.

'Why is there a pushchair here?' (Oh no! We'd forgotten the pushchair. What a give-away.)

'It's mine,' I squeaked, and I was thinking, *Nightmares are nothing to what I am going through right now*. Marsha's mum stood there, waiting for me to explain why I went around with a pushchair and, of course, I couldn't think of any possible reason on earth why I should.

My mouth opened and shut, but no noise, no explanation came out. Marsha wasn't any help either. She just stood there with a silly expression on her face.

A loud wail came from the front room.

'What was that? It sounded just like a baby.' True to form, Petal began giving her lungs a good work-out, yet again. Mrs Zewlinsky went straight to the front room.

'Poor little thing!' she cried, falling to her knees and gathering the infant to her chest. 'What in heaven's name is a baby doing here?'

It was at this point that Marsha's brain finally seemed to wear out completely and she lost all sense of reason.

'It's Rob's,' she said.

'Rob has a baby? He's only eleven!'

'No, no,' protested Marsha, going incredibly red. 'I don't mean – that.'

'Well, what do you mean?'

I took a deep breath. 'Can we sit down, Mrs Zewlinsky? I can explain everything.' Then Norman began hammering on the cellar door and yelling, and I could feel the entire world come crashing down around

me in a million billion fragments. Mrs
Zewlinsky strode out to the hall and
struggled with the cellar door key.

'Don't open that door!' I yelled. 'There's
an alien in there!'

'Don't be so stupid.'

'There is! You've got to believe us. We've
got Norman Vork in there. He's turning into
an alien. He's yellow and he's got poisonous
tentacles and . . .'

Mrs Zewlinsky at last yanked the door
open and Norman came staggering out,
blinking in the bright light of day.

He wasn't yellow, and he didn't have
tentacles, but he was angry.

Well, maybe *angry* is the wrong word here.
Imagine several hand grenades going off
inside a drainpipe, or a nuclear explosion in
the comfort of your own front room. Either
of those will do.

He was spitting mad. It took Mrs
Zewlinsky a good ten minutes to calm him
down, not to mention preventing him from
seizing Marsha and myself by the throat. As
soon as Marsha's mum had got Norman
under control, *she* went mad. Everything

had finally got too much for her.

'I have had enough of this alien nonsense,' she snapped, and she began strapping Petal into the pushchair. 'We are going straight over to Mr and Mrs Vork's and you can explain everything to *them*. I don't want to hear your silly stories any longer, Marsha, and you're just as bad, Robert. Come on!'

And we set off down the street. Norman pushed Petal. Marsha and I trailed along behind, while he kept turning round and smirking. As for Mrs Zewlinsky, she was still fuming away nicely behind us.

I couldn't believe it. We were being frog-marched slap-bang into the arms of the enemy. Mrs Zewlinsky banged on the Vorks' front door, while we waited beside her. From inside the house we could hear noises as someone, some *THING*, approached. We were knocking at the door, and Death was about to open it.

12 All Is Revealed

Death came in the shape of Mr Vork. His eyes fixed on Norman and the baby. 'Where have you two been?' he scowled. 'Your mother's been looking everywhere. We told you not to leave the house.'

'I'm afraid that these two have got something to do with that, Mr Vork. Do you mind if we come in? They've got a bit of explaining to do and something they want to tell you.' Without waiting to be asked, Marsha's mum pushed past him, into the little hall, and the rest of us followed.

'They shut me in the cellar, Dad,' snarled Norman. 'I couldn't get out.'

'You what!'

'Who's that?' cried Mrs Vork, hurrying through from the back of the house. 'There you are! Where have you been?'

'In a cellar,' growled Mr Vork.

'In a cellar?' Mrs Vork seemed mystified.

'They think your son's an alien from outer space,' sighed Mrs Zewlinsky.

'An alien?' Mrs Vork seemed even more mystified. 'Is it his ears?'

'An alien?' growled Mr Vork. His thick eyebrows had knitted together over his eyes, like mating caterpillars.

'I think we'd all better sit down while Marsha explains,' suggested Mrs Zewlinsky.

'Why me?'

Her mother pushed us through into the Vorks' front room. 'Just get on with it,' said Mrs Zewlinsky, and then caught her breath. 'My goodness, what a lot of computers and TVs and music systems. Are those mixing decks?'

'I'm in the business,' said Mr Vork, and his hairy caterpillars started crawling down the top of his nose.

'He does repairs, you know . . .' Mrs Vork's voice trailed away. Mrs Zewlinsky was staring at the electronic mountain. Of course, it was no surprise to Marsha and me. We'd seen it all before. The only difference was that in broad daylight it did look rather more ordinary, apart from the fact that there was so much of it.

Marsha seemed very taken with one particular television. From the doorway, Mr Vork watched everyone carefully. His eyes had gone into darting mode. Marsha straightened up.

'This television comes from our school. It's got our school name written on the side in indelible ink. That's so that nobody could steal it.' She gazed steadily at Mr Vork. 'But somebody did steal it, a few days ago, and now it's here.'

The silence this announcement produced fell into the room like a boulder dropped from outer space. (A silent boulder.) It was stunning. The only noise was the sound of my brain whirring inside my head as things began to make a new kind of sense to me.

Mr Vork's big body was blocking the door. He scowled back at Marsha and Mrs Zewlinsky. Mrs Vork began to whimper in the corner. 'The girl knows,' she whispered desperately. 'I knew this would happen. It always does. You and Norman, you can't stop . . .'

'Shut up!'

Mrs Zewlinsky's eyes widened. 'Then all this equipment here . . . it's all stolen.' Still Mr Vork didn't answer, and Marsha's mother moved towards the door. 'I'm going to call the police.' Mr Vork blocked her way.

'You're not going anywhere.'

'I beg your pardon?'

'Shut up and sit down.'

'What are we going to do?' whined Mrs Vork.

'We'll have to move on,' snapped her husband, 'like we did last time. But first of all we will have to fix this lot.'

'I've had enough of this,' cried Marsha's mum. 'Let us through.' She tried to get past, but Mr Vork gave her such a shove that she stumbled back across the room and collapsed into an armchair.

Marsha launched herself at Mr Vork, which would have been brave and wonderful if she hadn't done her usual party piece, and tripped over her own gangly legs. She fell at his feet and ended up beating her fists on his knees rather than his chest.

'Don't you dare touch my mother!'

Mr Vork laughed. It was horrible. It was the laugh of the Killer King from Krarrg. He was a very scary person giving off incredibly menacing vibes. I could almost see them shimmering round his hulk, like in some horror movie. His eyes looked as if a million volts of electricity were charging through them. This wasn't like Norman's little red *doot-doot-doots*. This was mega-phaser stuff: *Pyowww-pyowww-pyowww-pyowww*. I thought he was going to turn into an alien right there on the front room carpet. Except of course he wasn't an alien, as we now knew, to our cost.

I have to admit, I was impressed by Marsha's attack on Mr Vork. It was pretty brave.

'You can't keep us prisoners for ever,' I said, 'just because we know you've been thieving all over the place. How long are you going to hold us here?'

'Shut it! I've had it up to here with you lot.

Norman, you start taking the stuff out to the truck. It's round the back. Anyone makes a wrong move and that's it. You lot know too much for your own good.'

'What are you going to do with us?' asked Mrs Zewlinsky in a tired voice.

Mr Vork curled his lip. 'I'll think of something.'

Norman and his mother began carting TVs and computers out through the back of the house, while Mr Vork watched over us. At one point he told Norman to fetch the stuff from upstairs and several minutes later Norman came clumping back down, struggling under the weight of, guess what?

An alien.

There it was, and I mean, THERE IT WAS, in Norman's scraggy arms. Three legs, tentacles, poisonous frills – the whole lot.

You know what it was? A giant pot plant. It was some kind of big frilly green thing, stuck in a pointed pot that rested on a metal stand with three legs.

I think that was the lowest point I'd ever reached in my life. I just wanted to hide for a hundred years. Marsha and I glanced at each other and then quickly turned away. I don't know which of us felt the more embarrassed.

Silence descended. It was like waiting for the end of the day at school. You know how it almost gets to home-time and then the classroom clock seems to stop altogether? Time doesn't move forward at all, and you're waiting and waiting . . .

And then the window burst into a million fragments of glass and a man came hurtling through and landed on the carpet. 'Everyone freeze!' he yelled, and about time too.

I'd been waiting for this moment ever since I had contacted the police on the phone. (Ha! And all along you've been thinking what a wally I am.) I'd managed to unhook the Vorks' phone and press 999 while Marsha was making a lunge for Norman's dad and all eyes were on her. I knew I wouldn't actually be able to speak to the police without Mr Vork hearing, but I reckoned that if I could keep the channel open then they would hear the conversation, work out what was happening, and trace the call.

And that is almost it. Mr Vork was

overpowered. Waiting outside the house were half a dozen police cars and most of the neighbours, all agog with excitement. The police swarmed over the house and they found stolen goods in almost every room. There were three more potted aliens upstairs, and a load of other plants. Mr Vork had been doing over garden centres too. Apparently the plants were worth hundreds.

The police had been after Vork for months. When he was finally marched out of the house to a waiting police van, Mrs Parsloe almost went berserk. She tried to kick his shins as he went past.

'That's the one that attacked me yesterday! He put a blanket over me – you horrible man!'

'Everyone's mad round here,' muttered Mr Vork, shaking his head. Then he vanished into the van, closely followed by his son.

Norman had made everything up about being an alien and the photonic shield and all that. He had simply used my own fears to protect his dad. They were in it together, and Marsha and I had caught them. It was almost like *The Famous Five*, except there were only two of us, and we didn't have a dog, so it was even better.

Strange thing – when everyone at school heard about it they stopped calling Marsha 'Bogbrush'. As for me, I still worry and I still play the violin. (And I'm getting much better at both.) My pockets are still full of bandages. I mean, you never know when you might need an emergency nappy.

They haven't stopped calling me 'Chicken Licken' at school, but it's like a friendly joke now. They know I'm a worrier, and they also know I caught the Vorks. Even Kevin Durbell was impressed.

Anyhow, I like worrying. I had some spots come up this morning, red ones with a tiny yellow dot in the centre. I've looked them up in my encyclopedia and I reckon it's the first stage of Frobisher's Scrofula. All your skin flakes off and your bones fall apart. It's fatal of course. Marsha said that she'll look after me. She reckons that we're all aliens, all of us. You, me, her, everyone.

'How do you work that out?' I asked.

'I just mean that we all seem strange to everyone, except ourselves. You don't think you're peculiar, but lots of other people do. It's the same with me, and just about everyone. It's like we are aliens to each other.'

I screwed up my nose. 'You're weird,' I said.

Marsha's face broke into a huge smile and she chuckled. 'Exactly.'

Oh yes, you remember that sign Mr and Mrs Vork had on their throats? I saw it again, a few days later, on my computer screen. I was looking at Mystic Myrtle the Cosmic Turtle and she was doing next month's birthday sign. It was Gemini, the twins. The star pattern was identical. I knew I'd seen it somewhere before. I suppose Mr and Mrs Vork had each had the tattoo done in their lovey-dovey days. Not even Marsha had got that one.

And there's one other thing. If that wasn't a UFO over the Vorks' house that night, then what was it?